This book belongs to:

_____

STORYTIME AND FAVORITE RHYMES
Copyright © 2004 by Dalmatian Press, LLC

All rights reserved
Printed in China

FIRST EDITION

Designed by Emily Robertson

ISBN: 1-40370-527-5
12866-1103

05 06 07 LPU 10 9 8 7 6 5 4

Storytime

& favorite rhymes

Goldilocks & The Three Bears

Adapted by Bill Shockey
Illustrated by James Finch

Once upon a time there were three bears: a great big Papa Bear, a middle-sized Mama Bear, and a little Baby Bear.

One morning Mama Bear made some porridge for breakfast, but it was much too hot to eat. The three bears decided to go for a walk while their porridge cooled on the table.

Nearby in the forest, a young girl named Goldilocks became lost while she was picking flowers. As she wandered about, she saw the cozy little cottage that was the home of the three bears. She tried the front door and found that it was not locked.

Goldilocks entered the door and saw the three bowls of porridge on the table. "Oh, I am very hungry, and it smells so good," the little girl said out loud.

She tasted a spoonful of porridge from the big bowl and said, "This is much too hot!"

Then she took a bite from the middle bowl of porridge and said, "This is much too cold!"

Then she took a spoonful out of the smallest bowl. "Mmm," she said, "this one is just right," and she ate up all the porridge.

Goldilocks saw three chairs by the fireplace. She thought, "I am very tired and would like to rest by the warm fire."

First she sat in Papa Bear's chair. "This chair is much too big!" she cried. She next sat in Mama Bear's chair and said, "This chair is much too wide!"

Then she sat in the smallest chair that belonged to Baby Bear and said, "Oh, this chair is just right." Suddenly, the chair broke, and she fell to the floor with a bang!

Then Goldilocks thought, "I am very sleepy and would like to take a nap." She climbed the stairs to find a place to rest and found three beds.

She first tried Papa Bear's bed. "This bed is much too hard for me!" she said.

Then she tried Mama Bear's bed and said, "This bed is much too soft for me!"

Next, Goldilocks lay down on Baby Bear's bed. "Ah, this bed is just right," she said, and she fell fast asleep.

Just about this time, the three bears came home from their walk. They knew right away that someone had been in their cottage.

"Someone has been eating my porridge," said Papa Bear.
"Someone has been eating my porridge," said Mama Bear.

Baby Bear said, "Someone has been eating my porridge, and LOOK, now it is all gone!"

The three bears walked over to the fireplace.

"Someone has been sitting in my chair," said Papa Bear.

"Someone has been sitting in my chair," said Mama Bear.

Baby Bear said, "Someone has been sitting in my chair, and LOOK, now it is all broken!"

The three bears quietly went up the stairs. Papa Bear took one look at his bed and said, "Someone has been sleeping in my bed."

Mama Bear said, "Someone has been sleeping in my bed."

Baby Bear said, "Someone has been sleeping in my bed, and LOOK, there she is!"

Suddenly Goldilocks woke up from her nap and saw the three bears. She jumped out of the bed, went down the stairs as fast as she could, and ran right out the door.

And the three bears never saw Goldilocks again.

The End

Henny Penny

Adapted by Wallace C. Wadsworth
Illustrated by Nancy Speir

One day Henny Penny went into the woods to search for nuts. A big acorn fell from a tree and hit her feathered head.

"Cut-cut-cut-cut!" squawked poor Henny Penny. "Oh, goodness! The sky's a-falling, surely! I must go and tell the King!"

So she hurried along, and whom should she meet but
Ducky Lucky.

"Quack! Quack!" called Ducky Lucky. "Good morning, Henny
Penny. Where are you going this fine day?"

"Oh, deary me, Ducky Lucky!" cried Henny Penny. "I was in the woods gathering nuts, and a piece of the sky fell on my feathered head. I'm going to tell the King the sky's a-falling!"

"Oh, what a dreadful thing! Quack! Quack!" exclaimed Ducky Lucky. "May I come along with you?"

"Certainly," said Henny Penny. "We'll both go and tell the King."

So they hurried along, and whom should they meet but Goosey Loosey.

"Honk! Honk!" called out Goosey Loosey. "Where are the two of you going this fine day?"

"Oh, deary me, Goosey Loosey!" cried Ducky Lucky. "Henny Penny was in the woods gathering nuts, and a piece of the sky fell upon her feathered head. We're on our way to tell the King the sky's a-falling."

"Oh, what a dreadful thing! Honk! Honk!" exclaimed Goosey Loosey. "May I come along with you?"

"Certainly," said Ducky Lucky. "All three of us will go and tell the King."

So they hurried along, and whom should they meet but Gander Lander.

"Squonk! Squonk!" called Gander Lander. "Where are the three of you going this fine day?"

"Oh, deary me, Gander Lander!" cried Goosey Loosey. "Henny Penny was in the woods gathering nuts, and a piece of the sky fell upon her feathered head. We're on our way to tell the King the sky's a-falling."

"Oh, what a dreadful thing! Squonk! Squonk!" exclaimed Gander Lander. "May I come along with you?"

"Certainly," said Goosey Loosey. "All four of us will go and tell the King."

So they all hurried along, and whom should they meet but Turkey Lurkey.

"Gobble! Gobble!" called Turkey Lurkey, stretching out his long neck. "Where are the four of you going this fine day?"

"Oh, deary me, Turkey Lurkey!" cried Gander Lander. "Henny Penny was in the woods gathering nuts, and a piece of sky fell upon her feathered head. We're on our way to tell the King the sky's a-falling."

"Oh, what a dreadful thing! Gobble! Gobble!" exclaimed Turkey Lurkey. "May I come along with you?"

"Certainly," said Gander Lander. "All five of us will go and tell the King."

So they hurried along, and whom should they meet but Foxy Loxy!

"Good morning to you, my pretty friends," called Foxy Loxy, smiling slyly upon them all. "Where are the five of you going this fine day?"

"Oh, deary me, Foxy Loxy!" cried Turkey Lurkey. "Henny Penny was in the woods gathering nuts, and a piece of the sky fell upon her feathered head. We're on our way to tell the King the sky's a-falling."

STORYTIME & FAVORITE RHYMES

"Oh, what a dreadful thing!" exclaimed Foxy Loxy, but he smiled as though it might not be such a dreadful thing, after all. "Was Henny Penny standing near the big oak tree at the edge of the woods, may I ask?"

"That was just the place!" cried Henny Penny.

"Ah, I thought so," said Foxy Loxy. "I was there yesterday, and I thought the sky looked rather weak. The King should know about it. Are you sure that you know the way to the palace?"

The friends all looked at each other and shook their heads.

"Then I shall lead you to it," said Foxy Loxy, and he licked his lips hungrily. "Just follow me, and we'll all go and tell the King the sky's a-falling."

So Foxy Loxy led the way, and they soon came to a big hole that went beneath the roots of a tree.

Now this was really the door to Foxy Loxy's den, but he smiled and said, "This is a short way to the King's palace. I shall go in first, and you must follow me, one at a time. Then you will be in the presence of the King, to tell him the sky's a-falling."

Henny Penny and her friends agreed to do just as he had said. Foxy Loxy smiled slyly, and led the way into his burrow.

There he waited, thinking of what a fine dinner Henny Penny and her friends would make.

Henny Penny started toward the big hole. Then, all at once, she remembered something.

"Oh, goodness me!" she cried. "I have forgotten to lay my egg today! There are enough of you to go and tell the King without me."

Away went Henny Penny as fast as she could go. Ducky Lucky and Goosey Loosey and Gander Lander and Turkey Lurkey watched her go.

"Foxy Loxy knows the way to the King's palace," said Goosey Loosey. "Let *him* tell the King the sky's a-falling. I have my work to do, and I must get back to it at once."

"So must we," said all the others, and away they hurried.

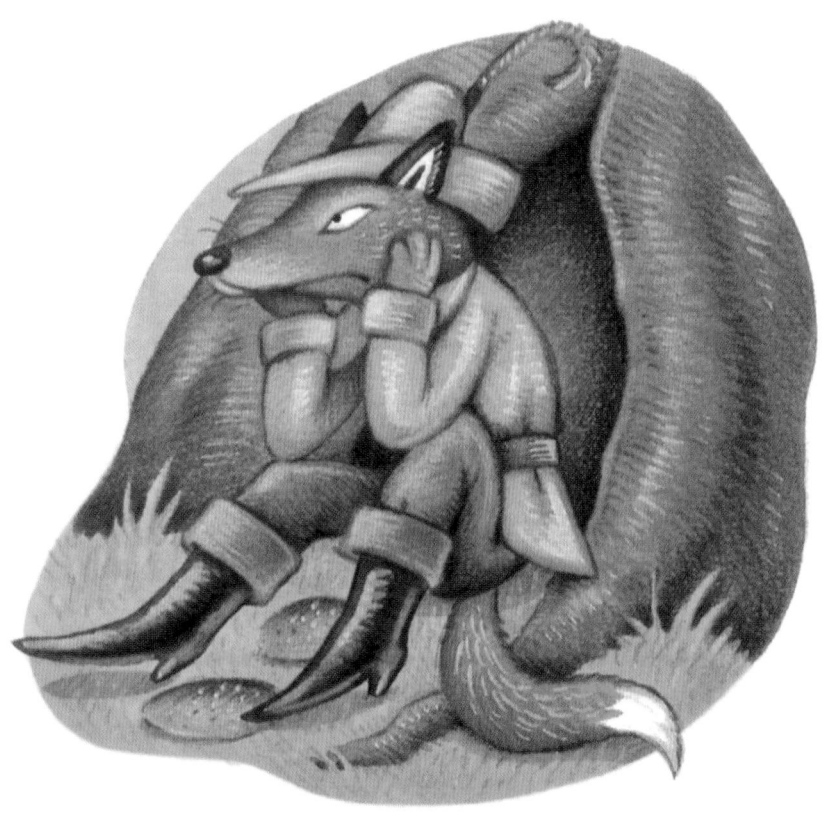

Foxy Loxy waited hungrily for Henny Penny and her friends to come. After awhile he came out to look for them. But they were gone, every one of them—Henny Penny and Ducky Lucky and Goosey Loosey and Gander Lander and Turkey Lurkey!

And so it was that sly Foxy Loxy had to go without his fine dinner and the King was never told that the sky was falling.

The End

Hansel & Gretel

A Grimm Tale
Adapted by Joe Loesch
Illustrated by Kevin Menck

Once upon a time there was a boy and girl named Hansel and Gretel. They lived with their father, a poor woodcutter, in a little house beside a forest. Often the family went to bed hungry because there was not enough food to eat.

One day the woodcutter took his children into the forest to gather wood.

Hansel and Gretel laughed and played so hard that they wandered from their father and were soon lost. Their father looked for them the rest of that day. Fortunately, Hansel had many of his favorite pebbles with him, and they had fallen to the ground one by one from the holes in his pockets. The children followed the path of shiny pebbles by moonlight back to their home. Their father was very happy to see them, but warned Hansel and Gretel to stay close to home and not to wander away.

A week later, the children went to play in the forest again. They did not heed their father's warning and wandered far from home, leaving a trail of bread crumbs behind them to follow back home.

But the bread crumbs were eaten by the birds in the forest. And so, Hansel and Gretel realized they were lost.

The children became tired and very hungry as they roamed through the forest.

Suddenly, there through the trees, they saw a strange little house made of cake and candy!

They ran to the house and began eating from it furiously. There were cake shingles and candy shutters. The windows were made of sugar. The flowers were lollipops.

As they started to take a bite from the chocolate door, it opened. Out stepped an old woman with a wart on her nose. "Who's eating my house?" she said. The children were startled at first, but the old lady seemed very kind.

Hansel and Gretel apologized for eating from her house. "We haven't eaten in such a long time," they said.

The old lady took them in and fed them some good wholesome food. "This will fatten you up!" she said slyly.

It wasn't long before the old lady's kindly spirit wore off. She snarled and ordered the children to work from morning 'til night. She had Gretel scrubbing floors and cleaning the oven. Hansel had to repair a broken table and gather heavy wood for the stove.

"Only a witch would act this way," Gretel told Hansel.

Still, the witch fed them well. Hansel and Gretel even gained a little weight.

One night, as the witch stoked the coals in her oven, Gretel heard her cackle, "Tonight I'll have Hansel and Gretel for dinner!"

At that, Gretel sneaked up behind the witch—and pushed her into the oven!

The witch was destroyed by the flames and the oven became
so hot that the house caught fire.

As Hansel and Gretel ran to the door, they came across chests full of gems and coins of gold. They gathered as much as they could into two potato sacks, and then fled from the house. They ran until they could run no further.

They sat beneath a tree to catch their breath. Suddenly they heard a voice call out, "Hansel! Gretel!" It was their father, who had been searching for them since the day they were lost. They ran to their father's loving embrace.

"Look, Father," Hansel exclaimed, opening a sack. "More gold than we've ever dreamed of! We'll never be hungry again!"

From that day on, Hansel and Gretel lived happily ever after
with their father in the little house beside the forest...
...and they never went wandering again.

The End

LITTLE RED RIDING HOOD

A Grimm Tale
Adapted by Ashley Crownover
Illustrated by Danny Brooks Dalby

Once upon a time there lived a girl who was called "Red Riding Hood" because of the bright red cloak she always wore.

One day her mother said, "Red Riding Hood, your grandmother has not been feeling well. Take this basket of food to her, and remember—the woods can be dangerous. Do not speak to strangers."

Red Riding Hood promised and set off for Grandmother's house. She had not gone far when suddenly a voice behind her said, "What brings such a bright girl to the woods today all alone?"

Red Riding Hood turned around, and there was a Wolf! But because she had never met a Wolf before, Red Riding Hood was not afraid.

"I am taking a basket to my grandmother," she said. "She hasn't been feeling well. We have such a good time when I visit; I'm hoping to make her feel better."

The Wolf nodded. "And Grandmother's house—where is that?" he asked.

"Why, it's only a little way ahead," she said, pointing. "Up around the bend and through the meadow."

Too late Red Riding Hood remembered her mother's warning. "Goodbye," she said.

"Goodbye," said the Wolf.

When Red Riding Hood was out of sight, the Wolf ran through the woods to Grandmother's house. He knocked on the door and a voice inside called, "Is that you, Red Riding Hood? Come in, my dear. The latchstring's out."

The Wolf entered quickly and rushed to Grandmother's bed. He snatched her up and pushed her into the closet. Then he put on her robe and kerchief and jumped into the bed.

Just then Red Riding Hood arrived at the cottage. She knocked on the door and called, "Grandmother, it's me, Red Riding Hood."

"Come in, my dear, the latchstring's out," said the Wolf in his best Grandmother voice.

Red Riding Hood pulled the latchstring and entered the dark room.

"Why, Grandmother," she said, "you don't look well at all. What big eyes you have!"

"All the better to see you with, my dear," said the Wolf.

"Oh, Grandmother, what big *ears* you have!" Red Riding Hood exclaimed.

"All the better to hear your sweet voice," the Wolf replied.

"And, dear Grandmother," Red Riding Hood said, "what big *teeth* you have!"

"All the better to eat you with, my dear!" snarled the Wolf, jumping out of bed.

At that moment Grandmother, who had finally recovered her senses, pushed open the closet door, waving a very large stick!

"Leave us alone, Wolf!" ordered Grandmother. "You should be ashamed of yourself!"

Suddenly the Wolf didn't feel hungry anymore. He felt bad for what he had done, and he dashed out the door.

"Grandmother!" Red Riding Hood exclaimed. She ran to her grandmother and hugged her.

The Wolf ran from the house in shame, and never threatened another human again.

The End

MOTHER GOOSE

Illustrated by Frederick Richardson

Old Mother Goose, when
   She wanted to wander,
Would ride through the air
   On a very fine gander.

Mother Goose had a house,
   'Twas built in a wood.
An owl at the door
   For a porter stood.

She had a son Jack,
   A plain-looking lad.
He was not very good,
   Nor yet very bad.

She sent him to market,
   A live goose he bought.
"Here, Mother," says he,
   "It will not go for nought."

Jack's goose and her gander
   Grew very fond.
They'd both eat together,
   Or swim in one pond.

Jack found one morning,
   As I have been told,
His goose had laid him
   An egg of pure gold.

Jack rode to his mother,
   The news for to tell.
She called him a good boy,
   And said it was well.

And Old Mother Goose
   The goose saddled soon,
And mounting its back,
   Flew up to the moon.

Old Mother Goose, when
She wanted to wander,
Would ride through the air
On a very fine gander.

A, B, C, D, E, F, G,
H, I, J, K, L, M, N, O, P,
Q, R, S, and T, U, V,
W, X, and Y and Z.
Now I've said my A, B, C,
Tell me what you think of me.

Little Miss Muffet
Sat on a tuffet,
Eating some curds and whey.
There came a great spider
That sat down beside her,
And frightened Miss Muffet away.

Hey diddle diddle,
The cat and the fiddle,
The cow jumped over the moon.
The little dog laughed
To see such craft,
And the dish ran away with the spoon.

Little Jack Horner
Sat in a corner,
Eating a Christmas pie.
He put in his thumb
And pulled out a plum,
And said, "Oh, what a good boy am I!"

How many days has my baby to play?
Saturday, Sunday, Monday,
Tuesday, Wednesday, Thursday, Friday,
Saturday, Sunday, Monday.

Mistress Mary, quite contrary,
How does your garden grow?
With silver bells and cockleshells
And pretty maids all in a row.

This little piggie went to market.
This little piggie stayed home.
This little piggie had roast beef.
This little piggie had none.
And this little piggie cried
"Wee, wee, wee!" all the way home.

I like little kitty, her coat is so warm,
And if I don't hurt her she'll do me no harm.
So I'll not pull her tail, not drive her away,
But kitty and I very gently will play.

Pat a cake, pat a cake, baker's man,
Make me a cake as fast as you can.
Roll it and pat it and mark it with B.
Put it in the oven for Baby and me.

Little Nanny Etticoat
In a white petticoat,
　　And a red nose.
The longer she stands,
　　The shorter she grows.

Little Bo-Peep has lost her sheep,
And can't tell where to find them.
Leave them alone, and they'll come home,
And bring their tails behind them.

Little Boy Blue, come blow your horn.
The sheep's in the meadow, the cow's in the corn.
What! Is this the way you mind your sheep,
Under the haystack fast asleep?

The End

Jack and the Beanstalk

Adapted by Ashley Crownover
Illustrated by David Wariner

Once upon a time there was a poor widow and her only son, Jack. Life was hard for them. At last, all Jack and his mother had left was their milking cow. One day Jack's mother said sadly, "Jack, you must take the cow to market and sell her. We have nothing left to eat."

Jack loved his cow and didn't want to sell her, but he knew there was no other choice. So he set out early the next day for market.

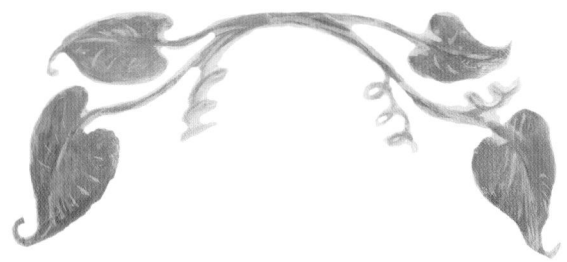

On the way, Jack met a strange old man who offered him five beautiful rainbow-colored beans in exchange for the cow. "They're magic!" the man said. Jack eagerly agreed to the trade.

Jack ran home to show his mother the wonderful beans. But when he told her what had happened, she was very angry. "Trading a cow for five worthless beans!" she said. "Now we'll starve!" She threw the beans out the window, and they both went to bed hungry.

When Jack woke the next morning, he found that an enormous beanstalk had sprung up outside the window. He quickly began to climb it, going higher and higher, until at last he reached the top.

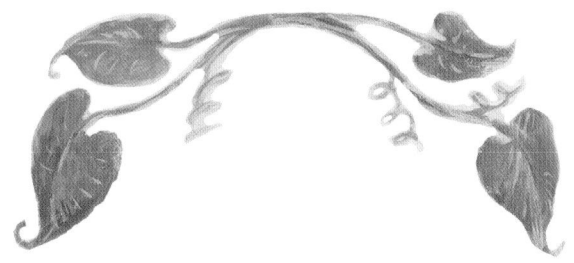

There Jack saw an enormous castle.

A woman answered the castle door, and Jack said, "I am very hungry. Can you give me something to eat?"

"No!" said the woman. "Go away! My husband, the Giant, will eat you!"

But Jack begged, and finally the Giant's wife let him in. Just then they heard a loud thump, thump, thump.

"He's coming!" the woman cried. "Hide in the oven!"

Jack jumped into the oven.

The Giant came in shouting, "Fee, fie, fo, fum. Look out, Human, here I come! Eyes, ears, hands and feet. I smell something good to eat!"

"Nonsense," said his wife.

The Giant sat down and called for his magic hen. "Lay!" he roared, and the hen laid a golden egg. Then the Giant dozed off.

Jack crept out of the oven, snatched up the hen, and ran away as fast as he could.

He climbed down the beanstalk and took the hen to his mother. Jack and his mother lived happily for a long time by selling the hen's golden eggs.

But it wasn't long before Jack decided to climb the beanstalk again to seek more treasures.

He returned to the castle and knocked on the big door.

"No," said the Giant's wife when she came to the door. "The last time I fed you, you stole my husband's hen."

But Jack begged, and the Giant's wife let him in. Just then they heard a loud thump, thump, thump.

"Quick!" said the Giant's wife. "Hide in this kettle!"

The Giant came in shouting, "Fee, fie, fo, fum. Look out, Human, here I come! Eyes, ears, hands and feet. I smell something good to eat!" "You're always saying that," his wife replied. "Come eat your supper."

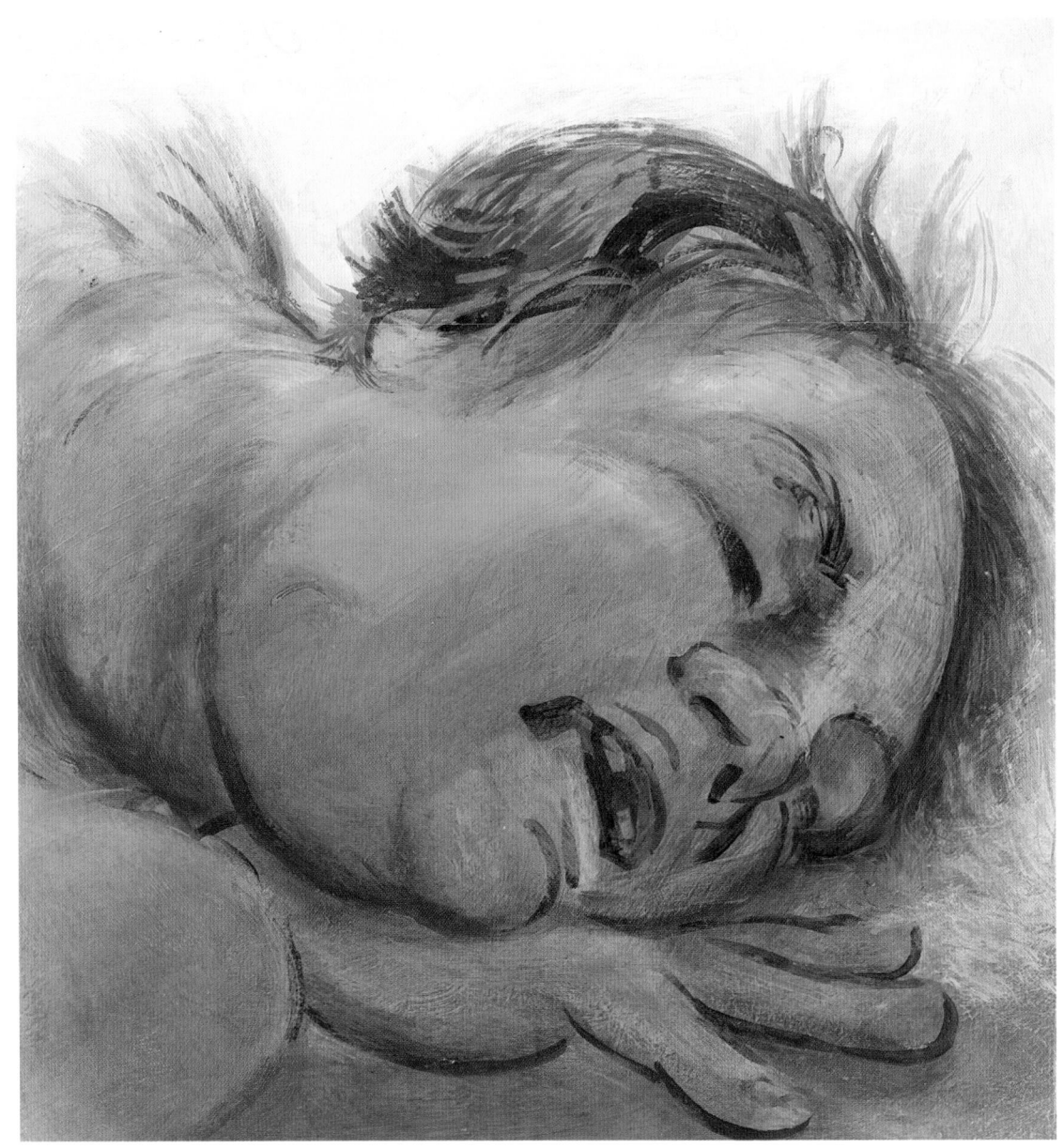

After supper, the Giant got out his enchanted harp. "Play!" commanded the Giant, and the golden harp began to play all by itself.

After a while, the Giant fell asleep, snoring loudly. Jack jumped out of the kettle and grabbed the harp. The harp cried out, "Master, Master!" The Giant awoke and ran after Jack.

Jack climbed down the beanstalk with the Giant close behind him.
As Jack neared the bottom he cried, "Mother! Bring the axe!"

Jack jumped to the ground and took the axe from his mother. He struck the beanstalk as hard as he could.

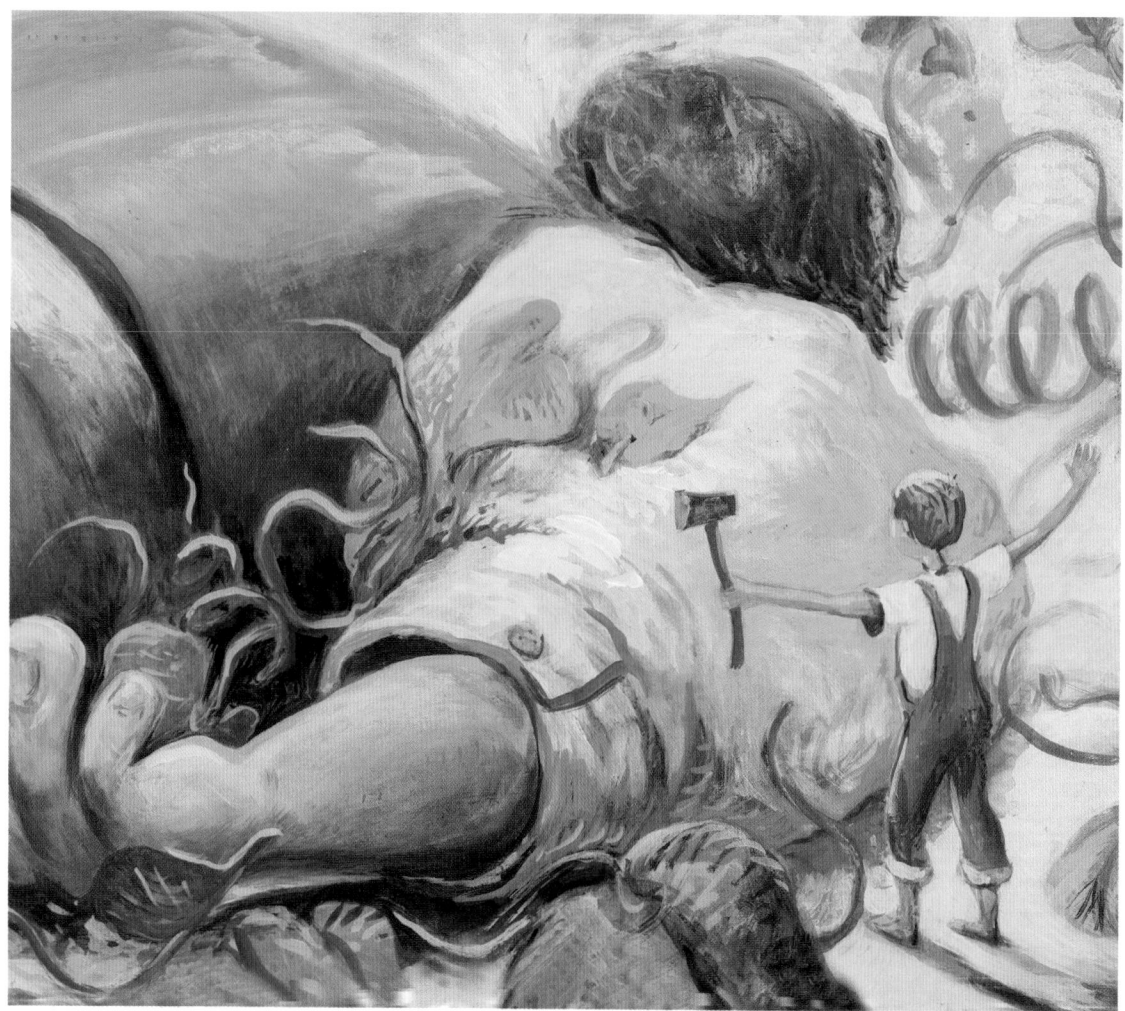

Down came the beanstalk, and down came the Giant—dead.
So all ended well for Jack and his mother, if not for the Giant.
As for the magical beanstalk, it never grew again.

The End

The Boy who Cried Wolf

An ÆSOP Fable
Adapted by Martha Stamps
Illustrated by Jeff Fuqua

Once there was a little shepherd boy with a big job. Every day he looked after his father's sheep as they grazed in the hills.

Although it wasn't difficult, his job was still important. There were wolves who lived in the hills, and their favorite meal was plump and juicy sheep. If he ever saw a wolf, the boy's special job was to blow his horn and cry, "Wolf! Wolf! Wolf!" Then his father and brothers would run up the hill and scare away the wolf.

The shepherd boy had been lucky and had never seen a wolf. But *he* didn't think he was so lucky. He grew bored watching the sheep. He wanted some excitement.

So one day, as the sheep were peacefully grazing, the shepherd boy blew on his horn and cried, "Wolf! Wolf! Wolf!"

He laughed when he saw his father and brothers running up the hill as fast as they could.

"Where is the wolf?" they demanded to know, panting from the hard run.

"I must have made a mistake," the little boy fibbed. "Perhaps I saw a rabbit running into the woods."

His father and brothers were glad that the shepherd and sheep were safe. His father said, "Son, it's very difficult for us to run all the way up here. Be sure that there really is trouble before you call for help." Then the men returned to their jobs.

"That was fun!" the boy thought. "They looked silly running up the hill!" He decided that as soon as the men got down the hill, he would play the same trick again. He blew his horn and cried, "Wolf! Wolf! Wolf!"

His father and brothers ran up the hill as fast as they could.

There was no wolf, and his brothers were angry. They didn't like being tricked. His father asked, "Do you know what happens to boys who make up stories and play tricks? Soon nobody believes anything they say."

"But it's not a story," the boy fibbed.

He laughed as the men went back down the hill. "Aren't I clever? I fooled them all!" He was so pleased with himself that he tried the trick again!

This time his brothers didn't want to run up the hill, but their father said, "He might be in trouble! We have to go!"

His father was sad to find that his boy had lied again. He could no longer trust his son.

The boy was still laughing when suddenly he heard the bleating of a lamb. He looked up just in time to see a wolf dragging the lamb into the woods. The shepherd blew on his horn and cried, "Wolf! Wolf! Wolf!" but no one came running. Even the boy's father didn't believe him this time.

All the shepherd boy could do was hide behind a tree as the wolf stole all of the sheep.

When night fell, the boy sadly made his way down the hill to his father, who cried, "Son, where are our sheep?"

"Didn't you hear me calling?" the pitiful shepherd asked. "There really was a wolf, and now he's eaten up all of our sheep!"

"We heard, but how could we believe you when you had lied to us before?"

"Oh, Father," cried the boy, "I did a terrible thing. Can you ever forgive me?"

"I will always forgive you, son. Losing our sheep is a stiff price to pay, but if you have learned the danger of playing pranks and telling lies, this is a lesson well learned."

The boy kissed his father and solemnly promised to always tell the truth. Never again did the boy tell a lie, and he became the very best shepherd in the entire land.

The End

THE
VELVETEEN RABBIT

Original story by Margery Williams
Adapted by Ashley Crownover
Illustrated by Pat Thompson

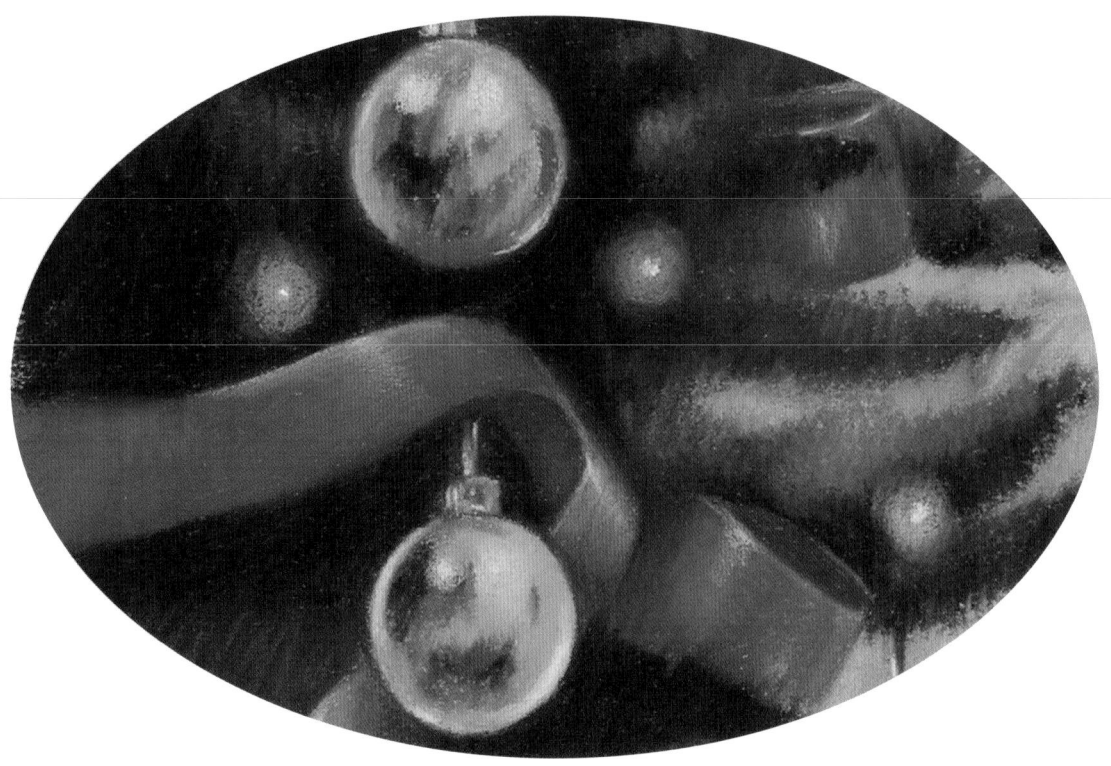

There was once a beautiful Velveteen Rabbit. His coat was spotted brown and white, and his ears were lined with pink satin. On Christmas morning he was the most wonderful gift in the Boy's stocking. All morning, the Boy played with him. Then in the excitement of looking at all the other presents, the Velveteen Rabbit was forgotten.

For a long time no one paid much attention to the Rabbit. The mechanical toys were rude to him because he was only a stuffed bunny. But the Play Horse, who had been there longer than any of the other toys—and knew all about toy magic—was very kind to the Rabbit.

One day the Rabbit asked the Play Horse, "What is Real? Does it mean having batteries or lights?"

"Real isn't how you are made," said the Play Horse. "It's a thing that happens to you. When a child really loves you, that is when you become Real."

One evening at bedtime, the Boy couldn't find the toy dog that slept with him, so his mother gave him the Rabbit instead. From then on, the Velveteen Rabbit slept with the Boy every night. The Boy would talk to him and they would play wonderful games—in whispers. The Rabbit slept snug and warm in the Boy's arms all night long.

Spring came, and wherever the Boy went, the Rabbit went, too. He had rides in the wheelbarrow and picnics on the grass. One day, he heard the Boy tell his mother, "My Bunny is Real. He's not a stuffed toy." That was the happiest day of the Rabbit's life.

After a while, the Velveteen Rabbit got raggedy from being loved so much. Some of his fur rubbed off and the pink in his ears turned gray, but the Boy didn't notice. He thought his Bunny was beautiful. When summer came, they played together in the woods almost every day.

Then one day, the Boy got very, very sick. The doctor said that all the toys in the room had to be tossed out because they were full of bad germs. The Boy got better, but the little Rabbit was put in a sack with other things and taken outside.

The Velveteen Rabbit wriggled his way to the top of the sack and looked out. Nearby he could see the woods where he and the Boy had played. He thought of how happy those times had been, and of how much the Boy had loved him. A tear trickled down his little shabby nose and fell to the ground.

Then a strange thing happened. Where the tear fell, a mysterious flower began to grow. It had emerald leaves and a beautiful golden blossom. The blossom opened and a fairy stepped out.

"I am the Toy Magic Fairy," she said. "I take care of the playthings that children have loved. When they are old and worn out, I make them Real."

"But wasn't I Real before?" the Rabbit asked.

The fairy said, "You were Real to the Boy because he loved you. Now you shall be Real to everyone."

In the meadow, the Velveteen Rabbit saw wild rabbits dancing with their shadows on the velvet grass.

"Run and play, little Rabbit," said the Toy Magic Fairy. "You are a Real Rabbit now."

Fall and winter passed. In the spring, when the days grew warm and sunny, the Boy went out to play. In the woods he saw two rabbits peeping at him from under a bush. One was gray. The other had brown and white spotted markings, a little soft nose, and bright round eyes that seemed familiar to the Boy.

"Why, he looks like my old Bunny who got lost when I was sick," the Boy thought.

He never knew that it really was his own Bunny, returning to look at the Boy who had first helped him to become Real.

The End

The Lovable UGLY DUCKLING

Original story by Hans Christian Andersen
Adapted by Kate Sullivan Watkins
Illustrated by James Finch

One bright, sunny morning in a corner of an old farmyard, a mother duck watched proudly as her ducklings hatched from their eggs. The five new ducklings were tiny and covered with soft, yellow feathers.

But the mother duck was puzzled because one egg did not hatch.
This egg was much larger than the others.

An old duck came waddling down the path and stopped to admire the new ducklings. "What's wrong with that egg?" the old duck asked.

"I don't know," the mother replied, "but for some reason, it just won't hatch."

The old duck looked carefully at the egg. "Well, that's a turkey egg," she said. "Leave it alone and go teach your new babies how to swim."

"No," said the mother duck. "I've taken care of this egg for this long. I will stay with it until the duckling hatches."

The mother duck continued to sit until the large egg began to wobble and crack. Finally, out came an unusual-looking baby bird. He was covered with rough, gray feathers, and he was much bigger than the other ducklings. His feet were large and clumsy, and his neck was long and skinny.

When the other birds in the farmyard saw him, they began to squawk. "What an ugly duckling!" honked the geese. "A very strange duckling indeed!" clucked the hens. Even the turkeys laughed at the new baby.

The poor baby duckling really did feel ugly. He made his way to a nearby lake to hide in the tall grass. He stayed hidden all summer long.

One night when the moon was shining brightly on the lake, the lonely duckling saw winged creatures gliding through the sky. Three magnificent swans cast graceful shadows as they flew through the night. The duckling stood still to admire them. Oh, how he longed to fly!

When winter came to the lake, the duckling grew cold and he had trouble finding food to eat.

One morning, the duckling slipped on the ice of the frozen lake. A kind farmer found him lying helpless and scared on the ice. The farmer wrapped him in his coat and carried him back to the nice, warm barn. The duckling stayed in the barn, and the farmer took care of him for the rest of the long, harsh winter.

Spring finally arrived, and the farmer led the duckling out of the barn. The duckling had grown. Feeling stronger than ever before, he flapped his wings gently in the warm light of the sun. To his surprise, he flew right off the ground into the bright sky.

He landed near some reeds at the edge of a peaceful pond. He could hear children playing nearby on the bank, and, once again, he saw the lovely swans. This time they were drifting through the water.

Afraid that they might laugh at him, the ugly duckling lowered his head in shame. As he looked down at the reflection in the still water, he saw another swan that was just as splendid as the others.

After a moment, he realized he was staring at his own reflection. He was amazed at how beautiful he had become. He was not an ugly duckling! In fact, he never had been a duckling at all, but a swan in the making. He glided into the water and joined the other swans. When the children saw him, they began to shout, "Look at the new swan. He is the most splendid of them all!"

He was not an ugly duckling, but a graceful and beautiful swan.
With this proud thought, his heart almost burst with happiness and joy.

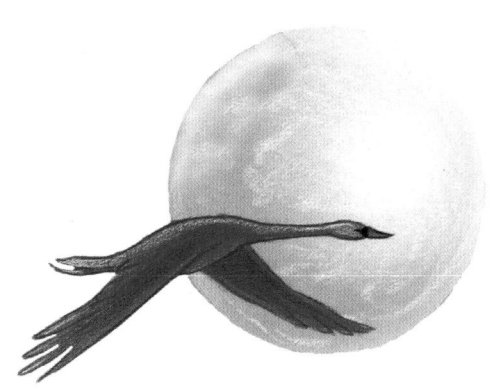

The End